Tan's Donuts

Chestnut Review Chapbooks, an imprint of Chestnut Review LLC
Ithaca, New York

https://chestnutreview.com
ISBN: 978-1-965158-10-4

Tan's Donuts

Maya Cheav

Chestnut Review Chapbooks

For all our Khmer grandmothers and grandfathers.

CONTENTS

Family Drawing by Matthew Sing

FRENCH CRULLER

I remember the moment your grandmother and I set foot on American soil. After years of misery, of being subjected to so much suffering during the war, we left everything we knew behind. I still have the naturalized oath of allegiance memorized. "I hereby declare, on oath, that I absolutely and entirely renounce and abjure all allegiance and fidelity to any foreign prince, potentate, state, or sovereignty, of whom or which I have heretofore been a subject or citizen; that I will support and defend the Constitution and laws of the United States of America." They got our last name wrong on the citizenship papers, though. After that, we were no longer the "Seangs," we were the "Sings." Then we needed work. What were our degrees worth when we didn't speak the language? Many of our friends and extended family who came to the U.S. seemed to be opening donut shops, so we settled on the same. Before we knew it, we had our own place in the center of the strip mall lot on Cedar and 14th. Our lives quickly became pink cardboard boxes and coffee with cream and sugar. I was manning the register when our first customer walked in: he was a 9-to-5 cubicle type in a blue button-up with his head buried in the daily newspaper. "French cruller, please." I rang him up, and he walked out, brown paper bag in hand. He left within seconds, the door chimes ringing on his way out, unaware that he had just made history.

GLAZED

I was a civil engineer in Phnom Penh when the war began. The Khmer Rouge devastated our home country. They targeted people who looked like me—glasses, uncalloused hands. They could tell I had an education, the type that would have been a threat to their ideologies. Truthfully, it was simpler than that. I couldn't see without my glasses, degree or not. I saw the soldiers herding people up and gunning them down. I threw my glasses to the ground and crushed them under my shoe, the glass shards crunching against the foam of my sandals. A soldier approached me, trying to read my face as my eyes bore a hole in the ground. "What do you do?" "I work on the farms," I said, praying none of our neighbors would rat me out. "Then why do your hands look so smooth? Looks like you've never picked up a shovel in your life." A fractal of glass cut through my shoe. "It's true! I walk so much in the fields that I bleed." I lifted my bloody foot towards his eyeline and he grimaced. He moved on to question someone else. For the next few years, everything farther than fifty feet away was blurry. Not long after we arrived in the United States, I went to the optometrist to get a new pair. He had me peer into a metal machine, switching through slides with the intent of having me choose which ones seemed clearer. At the end of my appointment, he poured dilation drops into my eyes, the world renounced with fuzz as your grandmother drove me home. When the haze went away, I saw a new world, one so different from my own, refracted through silver aviators. My optometrist is welcome at the shop for a free glazed donut anytime.

NOUM KONG

Your aunt, Mealea, was such a sweet child. By the age of five, she'd greet guests as soon as they came to the door, offering them a plate of rambutan and mangosteen before they even had a chance to sit down. She'd set the table and sweep the dining room without ever complaining. She was so different from your mother—timid, never the type to question authority. Her favorite food was noum kong, a traditional Khmer donut that looks like a big onion ring covered in sesame seeds. We made some every year for her birthday. She was about ten when the troops raided the town for the first time, soldiers marching through the streets, bearing AK-47s. I held onto your Yeh Yeh and Mealea with everything in me, her little hand knotted up in mine. We pushed our way through the crowd, screams flooding our ears and the sounds of gunshots reverberating in the distance. Somewhere in the flurry of things, I lost her. I hadn't noticed til we'd already escaped. After the soldiers had moved elsewhere, we searched all over for her, unsure if we would find our daughter or a corpse. Finding no one and nothing was far worse. I cried an ocean and a half, the tears crashing down my cheeks in waves, as a chasm the size of a black hole filled my belly. Your Yeh Yeh, on the other hand, made herself into a mountain. She knew we had to keep going or we were all going to die. After we fled to Thailand, we ran into one of our neighbors, Samnang, who told us that he'd seen Mealea a few weeks earlier. She stood amongst a group of children and soldiers, her face caked in dirt as she kneeled to the ground to place a circular landmine in a hole she had dug before covering it back up. When he understood what was happening, Samnang couldn't keep his terror in and gasped. She looked up and pointed at him, sending the soldiers to chase him down and open fire, but he managed to escape with only a few grazes. That was the last time anyone saw her alive. It's been decades since then, and yet the chasm in my belly is still there.

AMERICANO

Your mother was born a few years after we moved to the U.S. One day she came home from school crying, insisting we stop packing her durian for lunch because one of the boys in her class said it smelled like "garlic mixed with rotten eggs," and pinched his nose to ease the stench. She yanked out a red detention slip from her backpack that read, "disruptive lunch," signed by her teacher, Miss Lane. I told your mom to give her a coupon for a free donut and ask her to come in over the weekend so we could sort something out. Miss Lane came in wearing a perfectly pressed cardigan and a brown pencil skirt. She ordered an Americano with two sugars before telling me the smell of "that weird fruit" disturbed the classroom's lunch period, causing the kids to get rowdy and loud. She suggested I make peanut butter and jelly sandwiches instead. I pleaded with her, even offered her a month's worth of free donuts but she refused, insisting it "wasn't right" for her to make an exception for us and not the other kids in class who bring "normal" lunches. That very next Monday, she doubled down and gave your mom a whole week of detention. From then on, your mom didn't let us give her more durian, or any Khmer food for that matter. No more prahok or jackfruit, no more rambutan or lok lak eaten for dinner on our kathael. When she brought friends over, she'd roll the kathael up and shove it in the shoe closet, insisting we buy pizza.

APPLE FRITTER AND GINSENG TEA

Love, according to the movies your mother watched in high school, is serenading your girlfriend with a marching band on the soccer field, confessing your feelings with a boombox, slow dancing in an empty street. I don't think your grandmother and I ever felt that way about each other. Our parents were good friends and we were both eighteen, looking to get married soon—it was practical. We never bought each other teddy bears for Valentine's Day or wrote each other romantic letters tucked away in envelopes sealed with a kiss, but we ran that donut shop, co-commanders leading the troops. She made small talk with customers at the register while I threw batter into the fryers in the back. She'd iron my shirts when I woke up late for work and I'd do the dishes when she went to PTA meetings. When she was sick, I'd wake up a little early to bring her breakfast and tea from the shop before the workday started, and when I was stressed, she'd knead the knots out of my neck. She knew how to talk to your mother when I couldn't and she'd reassure me that my best was enough. I guess love can be an apple fritter and a cup of ginseng tea.

CHOCOLATE SPRINKLE

There was a family, four kids and a mother, who'd come in sporting bootleg designer shirts with copycat embroidery. Each Friday, they'd enjoy some glazed donuts, the mother sorting through bills while her kids ran around the shop playing with plastic dinosaurs and princess dolls. The youngest daughter's birthday was in September. On her big day, they came in, same as usual, but the mother bought her a chocolate sprinkle donut and whipped out a candle before singing "Happy Birthday." The eight-year-old pouted, complaining that they always got donuts, shouting, "I want a real cake!" The other kids joined in, chanting and kicking their feet on the legs of their chairs, starting a fuss that began to draw sideway glances from the other customers. I could see the mother's face crumbling from the inside as she tried her best to build a dam before the tears spilled out. There was a sunkenness about the woman's eyes that alluded to an unceasing ocean of grief, a depth to them that I was all too familiar with. I knew she didn't know how to explain to them that not every family has to spend hours couponing before back-to-school shopping or that the new shoes they got from "special visits from Santa" were actually from clothing drives. I knew she didn't know how to explain EBT cards or that they didn't ride the bus every day just to take the scenic route. It wasn't their fault and I'm sure she was more than aware of that. Your mom couldn't understand it either at that age. She took one sniffle and resumed her regular smile, drumming her fingers on the edge of their table as she said, "Alright, let's go get some cake!"

VANILLA LATTE

In high school, your mother would come into the shop sipping on a vanilla latte. Not one made by us, though, one from the Starbucks across the street, "Savannah" scrawled on the side of the plastic cup. That wasn't her actual name though, just what she called herself so kids could pronounce it. Your mother's real name, Sovannah, means "golden dream." That was what I wanted for her—to have all the things she could imagine and more. When the shop was finally doing well, we put her in ballet lessons, flute classes, and soccer practice. We pooled all the money that we had and put it in a college savings account. I wanted for her all the things I wanted for Mealea, the things she had never gotten to do because of the war. I knew she was meant for greatness and that all she needed was a little push in the right direction, but I think I pushed her too much. When she had mastered her pirouettes, I said her grand jetes needed work. When she was appointed junior varsity captain of the soccer team in her freshman year, I said she should strive for varsity. She was constantly foaming over from all the pressure I was putting on her. I hated how your mom's face scrunched up and got all soggy when it happened, maybe because it reminded me of what I looked like the last time I cried—the day your aunt disappeared. When your mother told me she was pregnant, I slapped her. It was the worst thing I ever did. I promised myself I'd never lay a hand on her again, and I followed through on that promise, but she made herself into a brick wall, a solid block of steel. She didn't accept any help from me, no offerings of money or baby formula, no quilted blankets or onesies, nothing other than letting me babysit you the first few years when you were growing up and even then she'd speak to your grandmother but ignore me. I thought eventually she would get over it. I shouldn't have been surprised when she left and never came back.

DONUT HOLES AND ORANGE JUICE

April 16th, 2005. 3:08 AM. That was the moment your mother walked through the door with you, our sweet Matthew, in her arms, bundled up in a baby blue blanket covered in ducks. Do you remember when your mom used to take you to the shop on the days she was working? Your favorite thing in the whole world was our donut holes, always eaten alongside freshly squeezed orange juice poured into your sippy cup. We were awestruck by you, sitting by the cash register, taking orders from customers. You couldn't pronounce your R's right, so "cinnamon roll" always came out like "cinnamon woll." Every other Saturday, we took you to the park in a stroller as you clung to your plush turtle, Shelly. We'd have a picnic on the grass, with strawberries and BLT sandwiches, and then we'd go to the playground. You loved going on the seesaw with me, laughing as you kicked up sand each time you pushed off the ground. The moment you showed me that drawing you had made of our family in kindergarten, I pinned it to the fridge. Every square inch of it is covered with pictures of you, ones with you playing at the beach in your flamingo floaties and ones at your third grade violin recital. I even printed out the ones your mom posted on Facebook from when you graduated high school. We thought about you every day after you and your mom left. You've gotten so tall now. Oh, chau, I've missed you.

MAPLE BAR

When your mother was in high school and she needed help with her world history homework, I remember her textbook having one singular sentence in it about Cambodia, in a section about the world's worst genocides: "In Cambodia during the 1970s, Pol Pot and the Khmer Rouge orchestrated the murder of three million people." The book fixated solely on our devastation and not on our joys. It didn't mention anything about Angkor Wat, a temple of hand-carved stone depicting our folklore and history, the eighth wonder of the world. It didn't mention that before the Khmer Rouge killed them, our country was home to painters and weavers, actors and musicians, our cities bursting with culture and beauty. My favorite Khmer singer was Sinn Sisamouth, the "King of Khmer music." I had a customer named Mabel who always ordered maple bars because they sounded like her name. Mabel was a bistro waitress by day and a jazz singer by night, playing walking bass lines while scatting to Aretha Franklin songs. She came around so often that once she invited me and your Yeh Yeh to one of her performances. The earthiness of her voice brought a smile to my face. It was a hard thing to swallow, the idea that Sinn Sisamouth and all the other musicians and artists died for something as simple as singing like Mabel did, something with the purpose of bringing people joy. No one knows exactly how Sinn Sisamouth died, but some people say that in his last moments against the regime, he asked to sing one final song, and he sang as beautifully as a songbird. The firing squad shot him down.

BLUEBERRY MUFFIN

The day I met Sunshine she told me she was going to be an astronaut. She was eight dressed in her teal green uniform and matching beret, covered in patches and pins of all kinds. She sat outside my shop at a plastic folding table adorned with brochures and cookie boxes, wearing a wide smile. Our regular customers would wake up hungry for a good donut, walk on over, then curtail to her table, stuff their bags full of cookies, and forget about me. The money went into a jar labeled in blue glitter glue that read, "future astronaut training funds!" In the rare moments when she didn't have people begging her to take their money, she would rifle through a variety of NASA brochures and astronaut history books from the library. Sometimes I heard her whispering the names of different spacecraft that had gone to the moon under her breath. "Pioneer, Luna, Ranger, Kosmos." She was awfully polite, always ordering a blueberry muffin from the shop. I could have sworn, though, that when she plucked the cash out of her money jar and handed it to me, she'd give me this mischievous smirk, one that read, "I'm gonna run you out of business one day." Who would think that my biggest competition in the strip mall would be a fourteen-year-old girl? Naturally, I learned how to survive in the growing market by having two-for-one specials every Thursday during each year's girl scout cookie season. I'd never admit it but I loved the competition, especially in the years after your Yeh Yeh died.

COCONUT

Depressed. I didn't understand what your mother meant when she told me that was how she felt. Sure, we're all sad sometimes, but what's a teenager got to be depressed about? Trigonometry homework? Who you're going to prom with? Everything your grandmother and I ever did was for her to have a chance at a better life. Lying on the ground between the corpses of our friends, pretending to be dead so the soldiers wouldn't shoot, tiptoeing through minefields holding our breath—it was all for her. We scrounged all our savings together for a business we didn't choose just so that she could have a better future. It was hard to hear that she was still unhappy. I didn't have the words to explain how I felt so I just screamed, throwing every English word I knew at her as she ran into her room and locked the door shut. I never had enough words for her. I didn't have enough patience either. After that, she started seeing your father, a boy from the grade above her. He wasn't the best influence. She started skipping classes and getting detention. The stack of missing homework assignments piled higher and higher. In the middle of her shift at the shop, your dad would breeze in, throw an arm over her, take a coconut donut from behind the counter without paying, and drive away in his unwashed car to who-knows-where. Then she flunked out of school, he left town, and well, you know the rest. You would think that losing one daughter would be enough to make a person kinder.

EVERYTHING

"I want to try everything on the menu." That's what the girl in the hospital bracelet said when she started with the plain cake and made her way through the fruity donuts and croissants. She didn't share much about herself, mostly only speaking of the donuts or the weather. I didn't even know her name. She never once cheated, never eating multiple items on the same day except for the last time she visited. Her eye bags had become canyon gorges, her face like the first snow of winter. She trudged into the shop, dragging her feet. The girl ordered the rest of the menu, sixteen different items ranging from our ham and cheese croissant to our vanilla latte. I watched there as she stuffed her face full, nose dappled in strawberry jelly, crumbs waterfalling over her chin. Then she said goodbye, cheerily, like any other day. There was a tremor in her voice, though, some semblance of an earthquake even she could not hide. I imagined her returning to a hospital, probably just like the one we're sitting in now. Liquid IV drips and lab coats. Freshly mopped linoleum floors and yellowed overhead lighting. The taste of chocolate cafeteria pudding and the smell of wilting flowers. That evening, I messaged your mother to let her know that I was dying. She never replied.

BOSTON CREAM

Althea was a woman in her eighties who wore floral frock dresses and loved a good Boston cream. She was gentle in the way she talked, her voice like a wind moving through the room. She came in every morning with a book in hand, always a hardcover. Adventures and mysteries were her favorite—she was particularly partial to the likes of Nancy Drew. Her favorite, though, had always been 20,000 Leagues Under the Sea. She'd make conversation with me, telling me about the crochet blankets she was working on or how the petunias in her garden were fairing. She dreamed of traveling out of the country, of hiking up glaciers in Iceland and swimming with sea turtles in the Galapagos. When she was young, she told herself to keep working, that she had to focus then and eventually she'd have the time and money to travel in the future. Her body had grown weary before she had the chance. Somewhere down the line, she came to need a cane, then a walker, and then a wheelchair. Her joints ached with each turn, the carpal tunnel twisting up her wrists like tangled chain links. One day, we caught word of news that there were dinosaur fossils found in a valley on the south side of town. She told me she was going to go down there herself to search for a tyrannosaurus spine. I laughed it off, of course, she could hardly even walk but a few weeks later, the archaeology team found her, fallen in. It sounds tragic, I know, but in a way, I was happy for her. She finally got her adventure.

CINNAMON TWIST

They'd come in, a group of skaters hurling profanities out of their mouths, with scraped knees and bruised forearms, but no helmets, never helmets. One of them wore a backpack, blasting punk music out of a speaker in the side pocket. I never played music in the store—I much preferred the quiet. He always ordered a cinnamon twist and would refer to me as "boss man." "How ya doing, boss man?" "Thanks, boss man!" For some reason, it bothered me. I'd roll my eyes at them and shoo them off as soon as they bought their food, the lot of them wheeling away through the door to do ollies and kick-turns in the parking lot. The boy with the speaker started hanging around the donut shop longer after his friends had gone home. He'd stay until the shop closed, asking me if I needed help taking out the trash, offering to tidy up the front counter when he could tell I was tired. Once I sat down and thought about it, I realized that those skater boys were loud, but never rude—taking up space, but never infringing on that of others. I had wasted so many years boiling over about things that didn't matter in the end. Time softens you, though, gentles your voice. After that, I started playing music on the speakers in the store. Some days it was Buddy Rich and other days it was Black Flag. It was too quiet without it.

OLD-FASHIONED

I started spending more time with Pu Dara after your yeh yeh
died. I'm not sure if you remember him—he's the one with a
stub for an arm. In his youth, he was charismatic—whenever we
were out on the town, he'd stop every five minutes because he
had run into someone he knew. Things changed after the war,
though. He'd told me stories of what it was like alone in the
war—how he'd lost half his right forearm and hand to a stray
mine, how he'd eaten live grasshoppers and scorpions to stay
alive. He says when he bites into potato chips now, he flinches,
expecting exoskeletons to crack out from under his teeth and
wings to flap frantically in his mouth. When he came to the
United States, he started working at a mechanic shop, always
coming back from work covered in grease and oil. We'd play
klah klok, a betting game with a mat with six symbols on it,
accompanied by a die with the same symbols: a rooster, fish,
prawn, tiger, crab, and gourd. To win the game, you must guess
which symbol the die will land on. One day, I bet $100 on fish
and won. Instead of asking for the money, I asked if he wanted
to man the register at the shop. We've been working together
ever since. He always comes in a few minutes late, throws an
apron on and grabs an old-fashioned donut from under the counter.

OATS AND HONEY GRANOLA BAR

Hmm, where do I begin? Actually, do you think you can get me a granola bar from the vending machine outside, first? I'm kind of hungry. Oh, wait you weren't supposed to write that part down, chau. And not that either. Okay well, I guess this is it then. Can you start on a new line?

Dear Sovannah,

How are you? Is work alright? How's your husband doing? Sorry for all the questions. I should slow down. It's just that I miss you.

Matthew is a good boy. You raised him well. Thank you for letting him come and visit. He's been here every day for the last few weeks. I don't know how he hasn't gotten sick of me yet but it's always a treat to see him after chemotherapy. I'll have to send him to the shop to have Pu Dara make him a box of donuts sometime. That's not why I'm writing to you, though.

The last day you spoke to me was the day of your mother's funeral. It was a strange thing to see—a mountain of a woman reduced to a bit of dust in a ceramic urn. You were carrying a bouquet of white orchids, wrapped in cellophane, Matthew at your side. It's engraved on the backside of my brain, the way you looked staring straight ahead at the urn, not afraid to show everyone else that your eyes were soggy from crying.

"I miss her, Pa," you said. I searched through all the caverns in my mind, trying to find something to comfort you, trying to find the right words to ease the pain but I didn't know what else to say besides, "Me too."

Yesterday, it hit me that the next time I see you again might be my own funeral.

I've sent you so many paragraphs, so many messages over Facebook, trying to speak to you and yet I don't think I've ever apologized. How silly, right? I couldn't bring myself to say one little word. Guess I really am as stubborn as people say.

I promise that I'm sorry for all of it. For how hard I made you work. For screaming at you, for making you cry. For not being able to understand you and not trying harder when I should've. I think that whenever I was mad at you, I was mostly just angry at myself. Your sister died because I couldn't hold on to her tight enough. Maybe that's why I held on to you so much.

It's funny, you know? Back then I didn't know enough English words to be able to talk to you. Now, after all these years, I've learned so much but I still don't know if there will ever be enough words to make this right. I know that what you want is to be left alone, but I just wanted to say all this now in case I never have the chance again. I am so proud to have you as my daughter.

With all the love I have left in me,
Pa

CHERRY TURNOVER

If you took one step out of my shop, you'd be greeted by the smell of acetone wafting over from Dawn's Nail Salon next door. She was a Vietnamese woman, the only other Asian who owned a store in the strip mall. She'd come in when things were slow, order a cherry turnover, and pull up a chair next to me while I scratched out a gold rush lotto with spare change from the register. When she bit down into her turnover, it oozed out over her red nails, goopy and glossy. One day, she straightened up her back and squared her face before saying, "My name is Duong, not Dawn, you know?" We had known each other for over a decade at this point and this was the first time I had heard this. "I wish I was as brave as you, not so quick to abandon my culture to fit in." I was grateful for the compliment, but in truth, I had questioned my choices so many times. I often wondered if being less Khmer would have made your mother's time at school easier, if changing the shop name from "Tan's" to "Tom's" would have gotten us more business. I didn't tell Duong any of this though, just nodded and sipped my tea.

PLAIN CAKE

The son came dressed in neon soccer jerseys and knee-high socks, covered in grass stains and sweat, while the dad sported a cap and khaki shorts. They only ever ate plain cake donuts, what one could argue was the healthiest item on the menu (for a donut shop that is), accompanied by a few tangerines and water. They would sit down for an hour and eat, while the dad peeled into the son, telling him all the plays he missed and why the angle of the shots he took were wrong. I could see his words eating away at the son, making him cave in on himself. The man reminded me a lot of my father. I had ten siblings growing up and he made all ten of us follow house rules. If you didn't finish your mathematics homework on time, you were beaten with a stick. If you spoke out of turn, you were beaten with his bare hands. None of these things were considered bad for a family of our culture at that time. Some days, the soccer dad would get worked up, biting back a scream, until he noticed the other patrons were watching with vulture eyes, ready to defend the child if anything happened. I knew there were plenty of times in your mother's childhood where I hadn't acted much different than that man, but I'd grown since then. I wanted to protect this kid too. You don't realize how horrible cruelty is when it's the only thing you've ever known.

LEMON-FILLED

I know smoking as someone in my condition isn't the smartest choice, but I like the taste of ash and menthol—I like thinking that my lungs are young enough to take it. I'd take my ten in the alley behind the shop, watching the raccoons ravage through the dumpsters as they fought over bags of baking powder residue and the remnants of a canola oil tin. One day, they weren't the only ones searching for something to eat. There was a girl who looked about eighteen with eyes that had heavy bags underneath them, so much so that she could have been mistaken for one of those raccoons. She was knees deep in aluminum cans and cardboard boxes fishing out a half-eaten lemon-filled donut when she saw me, uprighting herself. The girl had a strong jaw and an Adam's apple, hiding behind a thick head of hair so black it almost seemed artificial. "I can get you something else to eat if you'd like. It'd be a lot fresher than that." She stared at me for a second before nodding. Once she had some food in her, she softened up. Orion was a runaway from out of town, hitchhiking her way across state borders, jumping into the backs of trucks with her sights set on Los Angeles. She told me that she had people out there waiting for her. She said that anywhere was better than back at home—a home that felt like split lips and tasted like metal, a home that sounded like muffled screams seeping through cracks in bedroom doors. I felt an itch in the back of my throat, a deep-seated feeling of fear. Something inside me knew she wasn't going to make it out there on her own. I closed up shop for the weekend and drove her out, eating gas station sunflower seeds and shuffling through radio stations for six hours straight. A few weeks later Orion sent me a postcard of the Hollywood sign that read, in her chicken scratch, "Thanks for the ride!" Attached via paperclip was a fuzzy Polaroid picture of her and her friends holding up peace signs.

BEAR CLAW

The Donut Beast set up shop half a decade ago in the middle of
their nationwide expansion. I remember when they sent their
manager in. He had a snide look on his face like he was holding back a laugh, sporting his Donut Beast polo with pride. His
engraved metal name tag read, "Jimmy." Jimmy ordered a bear
claw and sat down at the table nearest to the register, cross-
ing a leg neatly over the other before taking one singular bite.
He chewed it carefully—tasting every component of its flavor
profile, studying its composition with meticulous precision.
Then he stood up, tossed the rest of the bear claw in the garbage,
and walked on out. He never came back so he must've thought
we weren't much of a threat. I guess he was right—business got
worse after that. How were two old men and a few stand mix-
ers supposed to compete with a coast-to-coast corporate chain?
They strung up their banners all across the lot. They'd hired
a guy to wear a pink sprinkle donut costume, spinning a sign
around in the early morning when the sun had just rolled out
of bed. Their marketing campaign took over the internet. Bill-
boards and bus stops, TV commercials and newspaper ads. You
would think they were running for president. And the construc-
tion—it took months. The power tools gnawed away at my ears,
their tiny hard hats sticking up over the fence line, always in my
peripheral vision.

BLACK COFFEE AND IRISH CREAM

Hartford and Corinna came in on Sunday mornings and ordered a black coffee and an Irish cream before sitting down to plan their wedding. She rifled through dress catalogs, sorting through a-lines and mermaid cuts, while he scrolled through potential venues. Would they be doing flower bouquets or gourmet chocolate bars for party favors? Was three tiers enough for the cake or did they need four to satisfy all the guests? They chipped away at it, week after week, planning each detail down to the seating arrangements and the kinds of utensils on each table. Their marriage must have landed on a Sunday because they came back here, tux, veil, and all, to get their regular order before going on their honeymoon to Versailles. You know, it's a terrible thing to find out your daughter is getting married through a Facebook post, to find out she went back to school to get her degree via an Instagram story. As if I'm some second cousin, twice removed, or a work acquaintance she's only met at an office holiday party. Like I'm not the one who's supposed to walk her down the aisle or the one who's supposed to take her graduation photos on her big day. I've sent her so many paragraphs, so many messages, trying to speak to her. I know she hates me and that this is all I get, but I just want to know one thing. Tell me, Matthew, is she happy?

STRAWBERRY AND CREAM CHEESE CROISSANT

That's what you can order for yourself when you miss your Tha Tha. Any decent donut shop would have it. They can be a bit tricky to execute, though, to make sure the croissants have just the right amount of flakiness and that the flavor of the strawberry jelly mixes with the cream cheese so it's not too sweet. It's one of the things I'll miss about this world. That and the people. I'll miss Pu Dara, all the customers who come to the shop, and your mother. And you, of course. You're a good kid, you know? I don't know many people who would have the patience to listen to an old man ramble on about his boring life. I'm sure you're going to do great in college since you've clearly got plenty of patience for all those long lectures. Your Yeh Yeh would be happy to see how much you've grown. As long as you try your best, you're going to do great. And even if you don't do that great, who cares! You're still amazing. And I'll never think anything less. Now you go home and you give your mom a big hug for me, alright? You tell her that she should post on her social media more often 'cause I like seeing the new things in her life. And tell that boss of hers to give her a raise, 'cause I'm sure she works way too—

Oh.

Sovannah.
You came.

NOUM ANSOM

I saw it in a dream—a lush plain by the Mekong River, in a time when it was not the color of dirt or filled with the contents of a landfill. Catfish swam among the shallows as a pod of Irrawaddy dolphins peeked up over the water. The entirety of the world was tinged with gold. Your grandmother was sitting cross-legged on a kathael, the blue and red reeds woven together in intricate patterns. She was setting out a plate, as the smell of banana wafted up through the wind. I had almost forgotten the taste of it, the sweetness of the sticky rice, the heartiness of the split mung beans. You and your mother stood under the tall fronds of a river palm, dancing to Sinn Sisamouth songs. And your aunt was there too, by the riverbed, searching for insects and amphibians of all kinds. She caught my gaze and her eyes turned into moons as she burst up over the grass, running up to me, and tugging my hand forward. She started laughing, her bangs bouncing up and down in the wind, our fingers laced together, squeezing tight. We were racing towards them, the stone pebbles and dew-laden grass beneath my bare feet. I was rushing up to your mother, ready to grab on to her and never let go, a tsunami of emotions flowing out of me, a melting pot of melancholy and elation all at once. Then I woke with a coughing fit, rising to the smell of distilled bleach and the sound of my heart monitor. There I was, in my scratchy hospital gown tucked into thin white sheets, missing the memory of something that never happened. I'll see your aunt and grandma soon enough.

ABOUT THE AUTHOR

Maya Cheav is a Cambodian-American writer and artist from Southern California, as well as the author of the poetry chapbook, LYKAIA (Bottlecap Press, 2023). Her poems and flash fiction have been featured in *Stone of Madness, ALOCASIA, Scapegoat Review, The Weaver, Across the Margin*, and elsewhere. Her work has received a Best Small Fictions Nomination. She was a top 10 finalist for the 2023 Palette Poetry Chapbook Prize, guest judged by Danez Smith, as well as a 2024 Tin House Workshop alum, under the faculty mentorship of Roy G. Guzmán. She is currently a 2024-2025 poet in residence with Collections of Transience.

ACKNOWLEDGEMENTS

The following pieces were previously published:

"Apple Fritter and Ginseng Tea" in *Collections of Transience.*
"Maple Bar," "Old-Fashioned," and "Noum Kong" in *The Insurgence.*

Support your local Khmer Donut Shops! Shoutouts to:

Donut King in Long Beach, CA
Donut King in Kailua and Kaimuki, HI
Donut Xpress in Conroy, TX
President's Donuts in Yorba Linda, CA
Tender Donuts in Stockton, CA